Arthur AND THE Sword

retold and illustrated by

ROBERT ⊕ SABUDA

ATHENEUM BOOKS FOR YOUNG READERS

Atheneum Books for Young Readers
An imprint of Simon & Schuster Children's Publishing Division
1230 Avenue of the Americas
New York, New York 10020

Book design by Ann Bobco
The text of this book is set in Caxton Book

First edition
Printed in the United States of America
10   9   8   7   6   5   4   3   2   1

Sabuda, Robert.
Arthur and the sword / Robert Sabuda. — 1st ed.
p.   cm.
Based on Sir Malory's tale.
Summary: In this retelling which features stained glass illustrations,
young Arthur proves himself to be the rightful heir to the throne by being
the only one able to pull the sword from the steel anvil.
ISBN 0-689-31987-8
1. Arthurian romances—Adaptations.   [1. Arthur, King.   2. Folklore—England.
3. Knights and knighthood—Folklore.]
I. Malory, Thomas, Sir, 15th cent.   Morte d'Arthur.   II. Title.
PZ8.1.S2134Art   1995
398.2'0942'02—dc20
[E]   95-9968

To my Auntie Joni
who shared some stained glass secrets
and for all the librarians who asked me to do this.

—R.S.

Long ago in the time of great darkness, a time without a king, there lived a fair boy called Arthur.

Each year at the time of the celebration of Christ's birth, Arthur rode with his family to the old church of Londontown. The Church was rough and dark and had stood on its holy spot longer than anyone could remember. There, before all the lords and ladies of the realm, the archbishop performed the High Mass for the Savior.

Each year the service was the same, at least it seemed that way to Arthur. But this time, in the middle of the ceremony, a great commotion arose outside. Suddenly a glorious light blazed through the ancient stained glass windows!

The worshippers rushed out to the snow covered churchyard and beheld a great marble stone. In the center of the stone, an anvil of steel held a marvelous sword buried almost to the hilt.

Arthur noticed that none of the swirling snow landed upon it, but merely passed over as if the sword was protected by an unseen hand. The sword seemed illuminated from within and shimmered brightly in the cold air.

The archbishop slowly approached the stone, his robes whispering across the snow. He read aloud the words inscribed in gold around the marble: WHOSO PULLETH OUT THIS SWORD OF THIS STONE AND ANVIL, IS RIGHTWISE BORN KING OF ALL ENGLAND. A king! If only it could be true, thought Arthur.

With the archbishop's blessing, each knight among the worshippers attempted to remove the sword. They gasped and strained until their faces turned crimson. But the sword could not be swayed. Arthur's older brother Kay was given a turn, but he, too, failed. Only Arthur's father, Sir Ector, and another old man who was hunched over and hidden beneath his cloak did not try.

No one thought to ask a boy like Arthur.

"He is not here," said the archbishop, "that can move the sword. This land still has no king."

Ten knights were placed about the sword to protect it until one who could take it was made known. The sad worshippers left the churchyard as quiet as the falling snow.

Word of the great sword spread quickly. Soon there were many knights, impatient for a chance to free it from the anvil's steely grip.

So for New Year's Day the archbishop called together a great jousting tournament. The most triumphant knights would have the archbishop's blessing to try the sword.

"And besides," said Arthur's father, "in a country without a king 'tis better for knights to play at the art of war than to make it." Arthur, his newly knighted brother Kay, and Sir Ector set out for London once again.

As they rode into town they passed the old church where the ten knights stood about the sword silent and unmoving, their breath turning white in the chilly air. Arthur watched them with wide eyes as his family made its way to their lodgings near the church.

That night, when the moon was high and silver, Arthur was awakened by a sound outside like the whispering of a stream.

From the front door of the inn he could see in the churchyard a hunched figure standing by the great sword but hidden by shadows. The knights guarding the sword were fast asleep and did not stir in the stranger's presence.

The bent figure took the sleeve of his tattered cloak and slowly moved it across the handle of the sword. He polished it and spoke softly in an unfamiliar tongue. The sword glowed even brighter, more brilliant than the moon above the church's steeple.

Arthur slowly closed the door and hurried back to the warmth of his bed.

The next day Arthur busily made preparations for Kay's first tournament as a knight. Upon arriving at the grounds he carefully shined Kay's mail to a shimmering luster. He made sure his tunic was bright and unblemished. And his sword. . . . His sword! Arthur had forgotten Kay's sword.

"How can I joust with no sword?" Kay cried. "Hasten back to the inn for it."

Arthur mounted his steed and raced back to town, his cloak billowing around him like a sail.

When he reached the inn he found it locked, for all had gone to watch the games. He beat on the door until his hands ached and his eyes filled with hot tears.

Then he heard the sound again. Like a stream. A whispering stream. Gently it began to snow.

Arthur turned and faced the churchyard and the great sword in the anvil. The ten knights were gone, having also left to partake in the jousting tournament.

The boy made his way to the churchyard and looked quickly to see that no one was about. Leaping up on the stone, he grasped the sword with both hands. The sound of the whispering stream grew louder until it seemed to fill the air with thunder.

Arthur closed his eyes and smoothly pulled the sword from the anvil.

When he arrived back at the grounds Arthur delivered the magnificent sword to his brother.

"It is not thine own but should serve as well," Arthur said.

Kay's eyes widened as he recognized the holy sword and hurried to tell his father.

"Sir, the sword of the stone has come to me," the brother cried, "therefore I must be king of this land!"

Sir Ector's face turned pale. He took hold of the great sword and hid it under his coat. He commanded Arthur and Kay to follow him back to the church.

When they arrived Sir Ector led them into the dark church, where an old man, shrouded in his ragged cloak sat in one pew.

"Kay," whispered his father, "put thy hand upon this holy book and swear to tell me how you came to have the sword of the stone."

"By my brother Arthur, sir," Kay replied, his voice shaking. "He brought it to me."

Sir Ector turned to Arthur.

"How came you by this sword, my child?" he asked.

"I . . . I had forgotten Kay's sword and returned to the inn, but it was locked," Arthur began. "I knew a knight could not be without one at his first tournament, so I . . ." Arthur's voice could hardly be heard. "I climbed upon the stone in the churchyard and pulled the sword from the anvil."

"Were there no knights at the stone to guard it?" Sir Ector asked.

"Nay, sir," whispered Arthur.

Sir Ector stood quietly for several moments. Then he led them out to the churchyard and bade Arthur to mount the stone and replace the sword in the anvil.

Arthur easily pushed it in. The sword appeared never to have been moved.

Then Sir Ector grasped the hilt and with all his strength tried to dislodge it, but could not. He called upon Kay to do the same, and he, too, failed.

"Now child," said Sir Ector, "show us."

Arthur waited for the sound of the stream but heard only the birds on the churchyard gate. The sword was already his. He removed it with one swift motion.

Sir Ector and Kay fell to their knees.

"Father," said Arthur, "why do you and Kay kneel before me?"

"Nay, Arthur," whispered Sir Ector, "it is not so that I am your father nor Kay your brother. For you are of a far higher blood than us both."

At that moment the old man emerged from the church. He rose tall and threw off his tattered garment. Arthur saw that he had flowing white hair and eyes that could pierce darkness.

"He speaks the truth, boy-king," said the figure. "You were born of the great King Uther and his queen, Ingraine. Your father bade me, Merlin, to deliver you to this good Lord Ector and his wife to foster as their own in

secrecy and safety until thy time was revealed. That time is now, King Arthur."

Sir Ector silently nodded in agreement.

"My lord," he said, "as my good king I ask nothing of you for my humble self, but only that you take on Kay as the steward of your lands."

"Dear father," said Arthur, "you and mother have taken me in as your own. If it be that I am king, you have only to ask of me and it shall be yours. I shall not fail you. I shall not fail this land."

So in the quiet of that day in the small churchyard, the young boy lofted the mighty sword, raising high the country out of darkness, and bringing forth a new world.

Notes from the Author

Arthur's sword was called *Excalibur,* which is thought to mean "To free from the stone." Arthur was made to pull the sword from the stone many times to prove to all that he was indeed king. But some did not believe that this 'beardless' boy could rule over such a great domain and made war against him. This was the first of many adventures that the legendary King Arthur would have. But is it a legend? Was there ever a *real* Arthur?

In about 950 A.D. a scholar wrote *Annales Cambriae,* which describes a battle that took place in 516 A.D. The *Annales* mention "the battle of Badon, in which Arthur bore the cross of our lord Jesus Christ on his shoulders for three days and three nights and the Britons were victorious." This is one of the first written accounts of Arthur.

In 1132 Geoffrey of Monmouth wrote *Historia Regum Britanniae* supposedly listing all the royalty of Great Britain. This is where a story of King Arthur appears for the first time.

In 1469 or 1470 Sir Thomas Malory wrote the most famous version of the King Arthur legend. Printed in 1485 under the title *Le Morte D'arthur,* it is based on French and English sources. The hero was no longer a sixth-century battler carrying a cross, but a great king transported to the era of medieval knights and beasts.

This book is based on Sir Thomas's tale.